Molly starts each day looking lovely and clean . . .

Molly's
dog Pip

. . . but it never ever lasts.

This week, Molly decides to practise staying neat and tidy because she is singing in the school show on Saturday . . . in a lovely new white dress.

On Monday, it rained.

Luckily I have my umbrella.

I've got water in my wellies.

I'm a soggy doggy.

The rain had stopped on Tuesday . . .

. . . so dodging the puddles on her scooter was a fun way for Molly to get to school.

I'm sure the teacher won't notice a bit of mud.

On Wednesday, Molly tried to bake some cakes,
wearing her apron to keep her dress spick and span.

On Thursday, Mum bought
Molly her favourite ice cream . . .

. . . the TRIPLE double-decker
with cherries and a dollop
of raspberry sauce.

Ooh,
triple
trouble!

Molly's only mistake on Friday . . .

. . . was not wearing her GREEN dress.

Come on Pip,
let's go home.

And now Saturday was here.
Molly loved her dress . . .

. . . and would try very VERY hard not to get messy.

Ok Pip, you can come but we are not going to the park.

Molly thought it was safer to leave the troublesome
scooter at home and walk to school.

An ice cream would be nice . . . but maybe not today.

She noticed the puddles . . .
just in time.

Molly was nearly
at school now, but . . .

WET
PAINT

. . . WATCH OUT!

Phew! That was close.

Molly had made it!

She was SO proud that she had managed to keep tip-top tidy.

Well . . . ALMOST!